William O. Stoddard

The Royal Decrees of Scanderoon

Dedicated by the author to the sachems of Tammany, and to the other

grand magnorums of Manhattan

William O. Stoddard

The Royal Decrees of Scanderoon
Dedicated by the author to the sachems of Tammany, and to the other grand magnorums of Manhattan

ISBN/EAN: 9783337410001

Printed in Europe, USA, Canada, Australia, Japan

Cover: Foto ©Andreas Hilbeck / pixelio.de

More available books at **www.hansebooks.com**

THE ROYAL

Decrees of Scanderoon.

DEDICATED BY THE AUTHOR

TO THE SACHEMS OF TAMMANY, AND TO THE OTHER
GRAND MAGNORUMS OF MANHATTAN.

NEW YORK:

Russells' American Steam Printing House,

28, 30, 32 CENTRE STREET.

——

1869.

SCANDEROON.

I.

ONE of the kings of Scanderoon,
　　Moses and David rolled in one,
　　Solomon-Solon of Scanderoon,
Was Hullaballoon.
Scanderoon is not in the moon,
But an island city, born of the sea,
And clasped in the wide arms of rivers three ;
A city with many a street and wall,
And many a palace and temple tall,
And thronging thousands, who buy and sell
In the marts of the city they love so well.
Thronging thousands, of every race,

Of every lingo and form and face,
In the sea-born city have found a place,
And all of them deem it their life's best boon
That Heaven has sent them to Scanderoon,
Under the rule, from June till June,
Of Hullaballoon,
Solomon-Solon of Scanderoon.

Mild is the sceptre above them held,
And never, by evil hearts impelled,
Have the loyal multitudes rebelled ;
But, now and then, as he sits in state,
In the shade of his golden palace gate,
Before the monarch his people wait,
To ask of his bounty the things they need,
And for help of his wonderful wisdom plead.

Dreamers and fools there of course will be
In such a city, born of the sea,
And they mutter their dreams as they walk their ways,
And they bother the king on his council days.
Ever he listens with gracious ear,
And his subjects bore him without a fear.

Bringing, with never a stay or stint,

The queer, crude things which they talk or print.

Ever he listens, with half-shut eyes—

The wonderful monarch, so good and **wise**—

As if the dreamers and fools could find

A flaw in the work of his kingly mind.

Every question he solves with ease,

And wise men come from beyond the seas

To listen and marvel at his decrees.

II.

NOW, on one of the council days,
The dreamers came in from their dreamy ways
To bother the king, as he sat in state
In the shade of his golden palace gate.

" Hear, oh monarch of Scanderoon,
We thy people demand a boon !
All of our lives would be perfect bliss
But for one grievance, for instance THIS :
All the tribes from beyond the seas
Come to our city just as they please,
Nor would we desire them to keep away,
And as long as they will we would have them stay,
But know, oh monarch, so wise and great,
That we deem it hard, when we come and wait
To speak with our king in his palace gate,

To find that his councillors of state,

The grand magnorums who round him stand,

Are all from some far away foreign land.

And the thing is a thing, oh king, that sours

On us all, to find that the city powers

Speak in a different tongue from ours,

And among our own ancestral towers

The royal favors descend in showers

On men whom the sea has washed ashore—

Men who never were washed before—

And we deem that now and then a boon

From the royal glory of Scanderoon

Should descend on one of the men whose birth

Happened this side of the rolling earth,

And not that all of thy gifts should be

To the driftwood that came from beyond the sea."

With half-shut eyes, but not asleep,

Sat the wise old king in council deep,

Until, with a wag of his mighty head,

He opened his lips and answering said :

"Dreamers and fools, the thing is so,

And a thing of evil it is, I know ;
My grand magnorums ought not to be
Of the people who come from beyond the sea—
People of every realm and race
And of every lingo and form and face—
But of them who from youth to age have grown
In this island city, and them alone.
Sour not, therefore, but live at ease,
And listen well to the king's decrees :

BECAUSE it is not right that they,
Who drift in on us from far away—
Some in the night and some in the day,
Some in the sunshine and some in the gales,
Some from the hovels and some from the jails—
Should sit in the halls of the king in state,
Or with him stand in his palace gate,

THEREFORE, from henceforth forevermore
The thing shall go on as it did before,
And every man who shall drift ashore—
Come he from hovel, or hole, or jail,
Come he in sunshine, or calm, or gale—

Shall straightway be girt with my robe of power,

Whether the girding be sweet or sour

To the dutiful people of Scanderoon,

And this is the king's decree and boon.

Scanderoon is not in the moon,

And here I am ruler from June till June,

Hullaballoon—

David and Moses rolled in one,

Wisest monarch under the sun,

Solomon-Solon of Scanderoon."

Back to their several works and ways,

Proud of their king and his council days,

In satisfied silence the people went,

Dreamers and fools, each one to his bent,

Glad that their island city alone

Could call such a ruler all its own.

III.

ET again from their dreamy ways,
On one of the great king's council days,
When, in all the pride of his pomp and state,
He sat in the shade of his palace gate,
While the grand magnorums that stood around
Hardly lifted their eyes from the ground,
The dreamers and fools a complaint must bring
To bother the peace of the wonderful king.

" Hear, oh monarch of Scanderoon,
We, thy people, demand a boon !
All of our lives would be perfect bliss
But for one grievance, for instance, THIS ·
We are of many faiths and creeds,
As each one thinks, or as each one needs ;
With different hearts we kneel or bow

Before the altars which we endow;

With different tongues we breathe in prayer,

Though we deem that the same God hears us there,

And we claim that all alike should be,

In the sight of our monarch, equal and free;

But the great magnorums that round you stand,

And speak in your ears, on either hand,

The purses of all make out to bleed

To fatten the priests of a single creed—

Men whom we do not hanker to feed;

And the thing is a thing, oh king, that sours

On us all, to find that the city powers,

The work we do and the cash we pay,

Go to build up the growing towers

Of one faith only, and all one way;

The great king's favors descend in showers

To foster a different creed from ours."

With half-shut eyes, but not asleep,

Sat the wise old king, in council deep,

Until, with a wag of his mighty head,

He opened his lips and answering said:

"Dreamers and fools, the thing is so,
And a thing of evil it is, I know;
For the wealth of the city ought not to feed
The hungry maw and the grasping greed
Of any one particular creed,
But all alike should share and share,
Or none at all—which would be as fair,
Or better, perhaps, for the purse of the king—
And ye do right your complaint to bring;
And the great magnorums that round me stand
Have shamed their monarch and wronged the land.
Sour not, therefore, but live at ease,
And listen well to the king's decrees:

BECAUSE religion should aye be free,
And the gifts of the king should equal be,
In case he should give of his own sweet will,
Or should button his purse, which is better still,

THEREFORE, henceforth and forevermore
The thing shall be as it was before,
And the great magnorums, young or old,
Shall be free to lavish the public gold
To build the towers and feed the priests,

SCANDEROON VOTING.

Whether in public or private feasts,

Of one faith only ; and while endures

My royal bounty, this course ensures

The growth of a different creed from yours ;

And that shall wax in its pomp and power,

Whether the thing be sweet or sour

To the dutiful people of Scanderoon,

And this is the king's decree and boon.

Scanderoon is not in the moon,

And here I am ruler from June till June,

Hullaballoon—

David and Moses rolled in one,

Wisest monarch under the sun,

Solomon-Solon of Scanderoon."

Back to their several works and ways,

Proud of their king and his council days,

In satisfied silence the people went,

Dreamers and fools, each one to his bent,

Glad that their island city alone

Could call such a ruler all its own.

IV.

YET again, from their dreamy ways,
    On one of the great king's council days,
    While he sat in the pride of his pomp and state
In the shade of his golden palace gate—
While his great magnorums, a mighty crowd,
In awe and wonder around him bowed—
The dreamers and fools made another complaint,
To bother the king—that royal saint.

" Hear, oh monarch of Scanderoon,
We, thy people, demand a boon !
All of our lives would be perfect bliss
But for one grievance, for instance, THIS :
Under thy hand, in the city wide,
Between the rivers on either side,
All the buildings that gather so thick,
Whether of stone or of wood or of brick,

And the earth beneath them, deep as you go,

Belong to the people, as well you know—

And in them we ply our works and ways,

And we bring to the king, on his council days,

Much of the gold which we gather by thrift,

With many a tug and with many a shift,

And, now and then, by a regular lift—

And glad are we when the good king smiles,

As he takes a look at his growing piles;

But the grand magnorums, who keep the keys

Of the public treasure, do as they please

With the gold we gather with thrift and care,

And none who pay it may hope for a share

In the good king's bounty : we bend our backs

To every load of excise and tax,

And all the while we know that it feeds

The foul desires and the slimy needs

Of a set of paupers, who never pay

A cent to the king, but who, day by day,

Fill their pockets and empty ours,

Aided by all the royal powers ;

And the thing is a thing, oh king, that sours

On the mind of the people, and so we beg

That the boot may be put on the other leg,
And the king may either keep his gold,
Or see it into the river rolled,
But not poured out, if the good king please,
For the lust of kites from beyond the seas."

With half-shut eyes, but not asleep,
Sat the wise old king, in council deep,
Until, with a wag of his mighty head,   •
He opened his lips and answering said :

"Dreamers and fools, the thing is so,
And a thing of evil it is, I know ;
The public treasure ought not to be
The spoil of paupers, nor scattered free,
To feed the lust or pamper the pride
Of the grand magnorums who wait beside
The king in state ; and the men who pay
The royal taxes should have their say
As to how the money is spent, and where
Shall be squandered the fruit of their thrift and care.
Sour not, therefore, but be at ease,
And listen well to the king's decrees:

BECAUSE it is wrong that the bending backs
Of those who labor and pay the tax
Should be burdened so heavily, all for those
Who neither can pay nor would, I suppose,
If they could—and who meanly and daintily shirk
Every species of thrift or work,

THEREFORE, henceforth and forevermore
The thing shall be as it was before,
And ye shall double and treble pay,
And heavier yet in every way
Shall the burden grow, till, one and all,
The palaces proud and the temples tall,
Whether of stone or of wood or of brick,
That over the city are built so thick,
Have all been handed over to me,
The king, as all of them ought to be,
And by me been lifted, hand over hand,
To the great magnorums that round me stand;
And with the houses shall go the power,
Whether the thing be sweet or sour
To the dutiful people of Scanderoon,
And this is the king's decree and boon.

Scanderoon is not in the moon,

And here I am ruler from June till June,

Hullaballoon—

David and Moses rolled in one,

Wisest monarch under the sun,

Solomon-Solon of Scanderoon."

Back to their several works and ways,

Proud of their king and his council days,

In satisfied silence the people went,

Dreamers and fools, each one to his bent.

Glad that their island city alone

Could call such a ruler all its own.

V.

ET again, from their works and ways,
  On one of the good king's council days,
  While he sat in the pride of his pomp and state
In the shade of his golden palace gate,
To bother the soul of the good old king
The dreamers and fools came up, to bring
Their weak complaint of another thing.

"Hear, oh monarch of Scanderoon,
We, thy people, demand a boon!
All of our lives would be perfect bliss
But for one grievance, for instance, THIS:
In the ancient laws of Scanderoon
(Scanderoon is not in the moon),

Written down in the years gone by,

In volumes on all of our shelves that lie,

Seldom opened just now, 'tis true,

Are maxims and rules nor bad nor few.

Murder and theft are forbidden there,

Rape and arson—crimes then rare—

And many another unpleasant thing

Are strictly forbid by the laws, oh king!

In those same volumes, huge and old,

Which the ancient wisdom and will unfold,

It is written, where all may read and see,

What the reward and pain shall be

Of those who shall dare the law to break,

Or any man's life or purse shall take,

Or the honor of woman, or set in a blaze

The homes where we live in our works and ways ;

But the great magnorums who round you stand,

And rule with the king on either hand,

Whether with or without a cause,

Have made strange work of the good old laws.

And the evil scum from beyond the seas,

Thick as the maggots in rotten cheese,

And the many devils who chance to be

Of this island city, born of the sea,
Shatter the things that are written down,
From end to end of our island town,
And, if by chance they arrested be,
Thy great magnorums set them free.
And the thing is a thing, oh king, that soun
On us all, to find that the city powers
Seem in league with the felons and thieves,
The dogs and pimps, and it greatly grieves
Our hearts to find that the good old laws
Are nullified, with or without a cause."

With half-shut eyes, but not asleep,
Sat the good old king, in council deep,
Until, with a wag of his mighty head,
He opened his lips and answering said :

" Dreamers and fools, the thing is so,
And a thing of evil it is, I know ;
They who the laws will overturn,
They who will murder, or steal, or burn,

Or plunder our women of what to them

Is dearer than aught in my diadem—

Plume, or gold, or glittering gem—

Whose evil courses deny all awe

To the will of God or to human law,

Ought to be met by the direst frown

Of the monarch who governs our sea-born town,

And punished sore, as it's written down.

Sour not, therefore, but live at ease,

And listen well to the king's decrees:

BECAUSE it **is** writ in the volumes old

That they who shall rob us of life or gold,

Of hope or honor, of home or gain,

For their evil doing shall suffer pain,

And all of the maxims of God and men

Are against such things, by word and pen,

And the bitterest thing that on earth may be

Comes to our souls when we daily see

The embodied devils of hell go free

To work their will on our goods and lives,

Our homes, our hopes, our daughters and wives,

THEREFORE, from henceforth forevermore
The thing shall be as it was before,
And all the rogues in the realm may know
The will of the king, that unwhipped they go!
And out of their number—they won't refuse—
The grand magnorums shall yearly choose
The greatest rascals for fraud and wit
In the shade of the palace gate to sit,
And do such justice on guile and wrong—
To punish the weak but not the strong—
As they may have learned in their own sweet ways,
And thus shall it be to the end of days;
And murder and theft, from this good hour,
Shall judgment deal by the l and of power,
Whether the thing be sweet or sour
To the dutiful people of Scanderoon,
And this is the king's decree and boon.
Scanderoon is not in the moon,
And here I am ruler from June till June,
Hullaballoon—
David and Moses rolled in one,
Wisest monarch under the sun,
Solomon-Solon of Scanderoon."

Back to their several works and ways,

Proud of their king and his council days,

In satisfied silence the people went,

Dreamers and fools, each one to his bent,

Glad that their island city alone

Could call such a ruler all its own.

LILIES.

VI.

YET again, from their dreamy ways,
On one of the good king's council days,
To bother the soul of the royal saint,
Came the dreamers and fools with a new complaint.

" Hear, oh monarch of Scanderoon,
We, thy people, demand a boon !
All of our lives would be perfect bliss
But for one grievance, for instance THIS :
Over our city, by day and night,
In the evening shades and the noon's broad light,
With a foul contempt of the law's control,
Rotten in body and rotten in soul,
Vile in heart as if fresh from hell,
Vile in their work—which they do so well—
Spreading corruption through will and brain,

Stirring disease into pulse and vein,

Whether in darkness or in day

Numberless harpies work alway.

Gamblers and harlots, hand in hand,

Like a ceaseless plague, infest the land.

Men, forgetting the name of truth,

Women, forgetting the shame of youth,

Flaunt and stalk through every street,

Poison the air which might else be sweet,

Poison the light of the beautiful day

With their evil presence and vile array;

And they wait, like evil beasts, for prey,

Where our children walk—our girls, our boys,

Our hearts' delight, our household joys—

To seize their souls and their bodies too,

To plague and poison them through and through,

And to drag them down in their halls of crime,

In their reeking lust and their moral slime,

To the hells of the harlots, before their time.

And the great magnorums who round you stand

With the gamblers and harlots are hand in hand,

And the thing is a thing, oh king, that sours

On us all, to find that the city powers,

And the might of our king, whom we love so well,
Are in league and covenant with hell."

With half-shut eyes, but not asleep,
Sat the wise old king, in council deep,
Until, with a wag of his mighty head,
He opened his lips and answering said :

"Dreamers and fools, the thing is so,
And a thing of evil it is, I know ;
Nor will my answer be dim or vague,
For who but the king shall stay the plague ?
Evil it is that your girls and boys—
Your hearts' delight and your household joys—
All the treasures you love so well,
Should but feed the greed of the fiends of hell ;
Evil it is that, just as they please,
The devil's own servants should sow disease
In the bodies and souls, in the hearts and brains—
Foul corruption in all the veins—
Of those who are young, and who should be pure,
And this disease is beyond all cure.
Evil it is that the thing should be

In this island city, born of the sea—
That the grand magnorums who round me stand
Should foster such a plague in the land.
Sour not, therefore, but live at ease,
And listen well to the king's decrees:

BECAUSE of the shame to our name and race,
The rotten disease and the foul disgrace,
The ruin of soul, and of body and purse,
The ruin that rots from worse to worse;

THEREFORE, from henceforth forevermore
The thing shall be as it was before ;
The gambler's lamp shall blaze at night,
With a hint of hell in its dull red light,
And ever, beside his well watched gate,
Shall the hungry daughters of Babylon wait,
And the great magnorums who round me stand
Shall feed their state with the fat of the land,
As it comes from the life of your girls and boys—
Your hearts' delight and your household joys—
And the young and the weak, who might else be pure,
Shall victims fall to the deadly lure,

And the body and soul shall know no cure ;

But the foolish and helpless you love so well

Shall be taught the filthiest road to hell ;

And the gamblers and harlots shall have all power,

Whether the thing be sweet or sour

To the dutiful people of Scanderoon,

And this is the king's decree and boon.

Scanderoon is not in the moon,

And here I am ruler from June till June,

Hullaballoon —

David and Moses rolled in one,

Wisest monarch under the sun,

Solomon-Solon of Scanderoon."

Back to their several works and ways,

Proud of their king and his council days,

In satisfied silence the people went,

Dreamers and fools, each one to his bent,

Glad that their island city alone

Could call such a ruler all its own.

VII.

ET again, from their dreamy ways,
   On one of the good king's council days,
   To bother the soul of the royal saint,
Came the dreamers and fools with a new complaint.

" Hear, oh monarch of Scanderoon,
We, thy people, demand a boon !
All of our lives would be perfect bliss
But for one grievance, for instance THIS :

Our city is born of the pure, blue sea,
And girt by the waters of rivers three—
Two of them large and one of them small—
And the ocean tides, as they rise and fall,
Wash the feet of our island town,
Swinging and plashing up and down

Easy it should be to keep us clean,
A city that lies such washings between;
Plenty of water and plenty of soap,
Plenty of shovels and hoes, we hope,
And other hose that may carry and squirt
Streams of water wherever there's dirt ;
And yet this town, that should be so clean,
Is the dirtiest city that ever was seen.
From end to end of each filthy street
Nothing is pure and nothing is sweet,
And the mire our rolling wheels that clogs
Is foul with the bodies of cats and dogs,
And the offal of cleaner brutes than they
Who leave our streets in so vile a way
In spite of all the money we pay.
For, know, oh monarch of Scanderoon,
That we, thy people, from June till June,
Pay enough, in our hard won gold,
Fairly counted and straightly told,
If into a sheet it was properly rolled,
To cover the pavement of stone and wood—
The pavement that is, we mean, that *should*
Be under the sloppy and slippery mire

Where our garments spoil and our horses tire—
From end to end of the city wide,
And leave an elegant fringe outside.
And the thing is a thing, oh king, that sours
On us all, to find that the city powers,
The grand magnorums who round you stand,
And take our money with greedy hand,
See no evil, or shame, or hurt
In leaving our streets all hid in the dirt."

With half-shut eyes, but not asleep,
Sat the wise old king, in council deep,
Until, with a wag of his mighty head,
He opened his lips and answering said :

"Dreamers and fools, the thing is so,
And a thing of evil it is, I know;
Evil it is that such filth should be
In an island city so near the sea,
And, worst of all, that the money paid
To keep us clean should be only made
The means of making us dirtier still,
Or be squandered right and left at the will

Of the great magnorums who serve the king,

And who round me stand in so grand a Ring.

Sour not, therefore, but live at ease,

And listen well to the king's decrees :

BECAUSE it is evil, and vile, and mean

That so grand a city cannot be clean,

With its piles of gold and its rivers wide,

And its long shores laved by the washing tide,

And because it is not for the public weal

That my grand magnorums should gobble and steal

All that the people pay to be neat,

In the way of cleaning each peopled street;

THEREFORE, henceforth and forevermore

The thing shall be as it was before,

And my great magnorums may hog the gold,

And the people struggle through dirt untold,

And in all the city, born of the sea,

The filth, and stench, and carrion be

A sign of the garbage in human shape—

Not the form of a glorified ape—

That around me loafs on every side

When I in my palace gate abide ;

When the grand magnorums about me stand

To council the king, on either hand—

And dirt shall be the seal of my power,

Whether the thing be sweet or sour

To the dutiful people of Scanderoon,

And this is the king's decree and boon.

Scanderoon is not in the moon,

And here I am ruler from June till June,

Hullaballoon—

David and Moses rolled in one,

Wisest monarch under the sun,

Solomon-Solon of Scanderoon."

Back to their several works and ways,

Proud of their king and his council days,

In satisfied silence the people went,

Dreamers and fools, each one to his bent,

Glad that their island city alone

Could call such a ruler all its own.

VIII.

YET again, from their dreamy ways,
On one of the good king's council days,
To bother the soul of the royal saint,
Came the dreamers and fools with a new complaint.

" Hear, oh monarch of Scanderoon,
We, thy people, demand a boon !
All of our lives would be perfect bliss
But for one grievance, for instance THIS :
In love and honor we all agree
For our island city, born of the sea,
In love for every street and wall,
For every palace and temple tall,
For all of its works and all of its ways,
And our love has grown for these many days.

We love our laws and we love our king,

And to him our tribute we gladly bring ;

But know, oh monarch, so wise and great,

That here, in the shade of thy palace gate,

Are many things done such love to cool

In the heart of every dreamer and fool.

We began to Justice a shrine to build,

In the years gone by, and thy people willed

That in it, so long as the city stood,

Should be done the things that were right and good .

That there, with learning, and truth, and wit,

The good king's judges might daily sit,

To hear the cause of the rich and poor,

And to all of thy people the right insure.

Slowly the temple's walls have grown

In the strength of iron, and glass, and stone,

But its growth is hindered on every hand

By the great magnorums who round you stand ;

And for every dollar of tribute spent

To build, in the people's good intent,

Five must go to fill the purse

Of the great magnorums ; and, what is worse,

Even the judges we hoped would sit

JUSTICE.

To deal out learning, and truth, and wit,

Have gone, like the temple, into the hand

Of the merciless crew who around you stand.

And, now that the truth to the king is told,

For every ounce of justice doled

To the rich or the poor, we must give our gold

In a treble weight, and even then,

From the hands of these evil and greedy men,

The kind of justice is queer and low,

And comes, like the temple-building, *slow ;*

And ever there lingers a dismal stench

Of fraud and guile around every bench,

Whether of iron, or wood, or stone,

Where they, whom thy grand magnorums own,

In the very light of the king's own eye,

Frown on us all when we come to buy.

And the thing is a thing, oh king, that sours

On us all, when we find that the city powers,

The public right, and the public purse

Are rotting away with so foul a curse—

That truth is trampled and wrong is wrought,

And the cause of the poor is sold and bought."

With half-shut eyes, but not asleep,
Sat the wise old king, in council deep,
Until, with a wag of his mighty head,
He opened his lips and answering said :

"Dreamers and fools, the thing is so,
And a thing of evil it is, I know ;
Right and justice should aye be free
In this island city, born of the sea ;
And when, in their various works and ways,
My dutiful people desire to raise
A temple to Justice, their tribute gold
Should be fairly spent and justly told.
Nor does four fifths of it all belong
To my grand magnorums, many and strong ;
And the price of a judge should be never so high
That a poor man cannot come up and buy.
Sour not, therefore, but live at ease,
And listen well to the king's decrees :

BECAUSE the curse of a venal court,
Of truth the shame and of rogues the sport,

Is one that God himself offends,

And the worst that the devil ever sends

To hurt the just and to serve the ends

Of the vilest tools that to sin he lends,

THEREFORE, from henceforth forevermore

The thing shall be as it was before ;

In a steadier stream the gold shall flow,

And the temple more slowly than ever grow—

A hateful sight in the eyes of the good—

And the iron, the glass, the stone, the wood

Shall witnesses all of the justice be

That is done in this city, born of the sea ;

And every cause that is won or lost

Shall gather a heavier shame and cost,

And the price of a judge shall be more and more,

And the bench shall stink with a stench as sore

As that which arose from Sodom of old

When the kind of justice you buy is doled ;

Each grand magnorum a judge shall own,

And every judge shall be overthrown

Who dares to give what he ought to sell,

Or the poor protect, or a bribe repel ;

The greater his greed the greater his power,

Whether the thing be sweet or sour

To the dutiful people of Scanderoon,

And this is the king's decree and boon.

Scanderoon is not in the moon,

And here I am ruler from June till June,

Hullaballoon —

David and Moses rolled in one,

Wisest monarch under the sun,

Solomon-Solon of Scanderoon."

Back to their several works and ways,

Proud of their king and his council days,

In satisfied silence the people went,

Dreamers and fools, each one to his bent,

Glad that their island city alone

Could call such a ruler all its own.

IX.

ET again, from their dreamy ways,

On one of the good king's council days,

To bother the soul of the royal saint,

Come the dreamers and fools with a new complaint.

" Hear, oh monarch of Scanderoon,

We, thy people, demand a boon !

All of our lives would be perfect bliss,

But for one grievance, for instance THIS :

By the good old laws, which are still in force

Under the king, as a matter of course,

Fairly and well it is written down

How thy people shall manage the town

In the best and easiest way, and still

Be loyal and true to the royal will.

Doubtless the king knows it all by rote,

About our right to come up and vote

Who shall as grand magnorums stand

By the side of the king, on either hand,

And live on his bounty year by year,

And the right is a right we all hold dear.

Now the king and the grand magnorums please

That the men who come from beyond the seas,

Of every nation, and lingo and face,

Should also vote, by special grace ;

And though they are neither wise nor few,

This matter pleases thy people, too.

The men from the countries far away,

Provided only they come to stay

And behave themselves in a decent way,

Are welcome as summer to come and vote,

And every hurrah from a foreign throat

Sounds as well in the popular ear

As if it came with an accent clear

Of any trace of a foreign tongue,

Or rose in the strength of a native lung.

But know, oh monarch, so wise and good,

That one thing goes as it never should :

Ever and aye as they come ashore,

Thousand on thousand, more and more,

In crowds that are never clean or thin,

The grand magnorums rake them in.

Their hearts they twist, and their ears they fill,

And their bellies, too; and to work their will

They teach them lies of every hue

Concerning the king.   Oh, king, 'tis true!

They bring them so to the polls; and then,

For every vote of the loyal men,

The grand magnorum slips in ten.

The votes of the men beyond the seas

Are many; but, not content with these,

Our rights as voters they override,

As if the law in the books had lied,

Or their own sweet souls had been multiplied.

And the thing is a thing, oh king, that sours

On us all, to find that the city powers,

By the aid of the men from beyond the seas,

Are from us reft by such deeds as these.

With half-shut eyes, but not asleep,

Sat the good old king, in council deep,

Until, with a wag of his mighty head,
He opened his lips and answering said:

" Dreamers and fools, the thing is so,
And a thing of evil it is, I know;
There should be but one voice for each man's throat;
And for each man's will but a single vote.
'Tis a scandalous thing in the eyes of men
That any magnorum should count for ten,
Or that those who come from beyond the seas
Should vote as many times as they please.
The city can never be safe or strong
While its rulers are chosen by guile and wrong.
Sour not, therefore, but live at ease,
And listen well to the king's decrees:

Because, in the volumes good and old,
The law of the voter is wisely told,
And because it is right, and fair, and just
That they who count should be true to their trust,
Nor should keep on voting themselves, for fun,
When the polls are closed and the day is done,
And all of the people who count *for one*
Have given it up with the setting sun;

THEREFORE, henceforth and forevermore
The thing shall be as it was before;
The men who come from beyond the seas
Shall vote as many times as they please,
Whether they come to our town to stay—
For the good of some fair land far away—
Or whether only ashore for a day;
And my grand magnorums, those mighty men,
Shall multiply yearly, ten by ten,
And keep on voting by candle-light
When the day is done, and the kindly night
Covers away from the popular sight
The deed that murders their dearest right.
And with the votes shall go the power,
Whether the thing be sweet or sour
To the dutiful people of Scanderoon,
And this is the king's decree and boon.
Scanderoon is not in the moon,
And here I am ruler from June till June,
Hullaballoon—
David and Moses rolled in one,
Wisest monarch under the sun,
Solomon-Solon of Scanderoon."

COUNSEL.